Adap...

x

Designed by Helen Cooke
Edited by Jenny Tyler
Reading consultants: Alison Kelly and Anne Washtell

There is ... very page.

Ted likes tea and cake and red.

One day, beside his bright red shed...
a clever plan pops in his head.

He runs inside and makes a drawing.

"I think I'll need to do some sawing."

But first he needs help with his bed.
He wants it in his bright red shed.

Ted smiles and finds his saw. (It's red!)

Pup barks, "What are you up to, Ted?"

Ted starts to saw. "Ahh, wait and see.
Be patient while I cut this tree."

Ted counts the slices. "I need four."

One, two, three... so just one more!

Now Ted must hammer.
"I need a nail!"

But the nail jar only has a snail.

Pup peers in pots.
"Where are the nails?"

Look! What's that on the mice's tails?

Ted calls his friends to help him out.
"What are you doing?" Penguin pouts.

Ted puffs and pants. "We're nearly done and then you'll see. It's lots of fun."

Now Penguin gets Ted's clever plan.
They set off...

...in his
caravan!

Puzzles

Puzzle 1
What is Ted doing? Match the word to the picture.

smiling	sitting	sawing

Puzzle 2
Which words rhyme with Ted?

Penguin   shed   Pup
head   hammer   red
cake   bed   mice

Puzzle 3
Choose the right speech bubble for the picture.

Puzzle 4
Spot the six differences between the two pictures.

Answers to puzzles

Puzzle 1

| sawing | smiling | sitting |

Puzzle 2
These words rhyme with Ted:

shed

head

red

bed

Puzzle 3

Puzzle 4

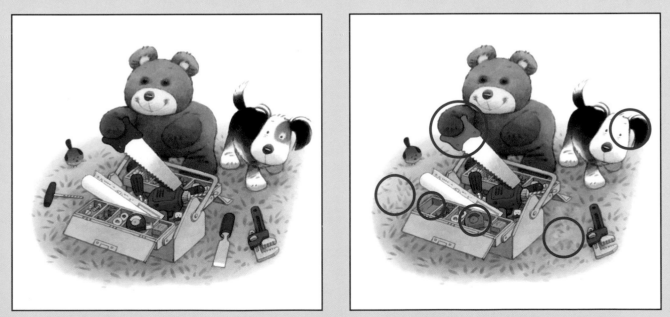

About phonics

Phonics is a method of teaching reading used extensively in today's schools. At its heart is an emphasis on identifying the *sounds* of letters, or combinations of letters, that are then put together to make words. These sounds are known as phonemes.

Starting to read

Learning to read is an important milestone for any child. The process can begin well before children start to learn letters and put them together to read words. The sooner children can discover books and enjoy stories and language, the better they will be prepared for reading themselves, first with the help of an adult and then independently.

You can find out more about phonics on the Usborne Very First Reading website, **usborne.com/veryfirstreading** (US readers go to **veryfirstreading.com**). Click on the **Parents** tab at the top of the page, then scroll down and click on **About synthetic phonics**.

Phonemic awareness

An important early stage in pre-reading and early reading is developing phonemic awareness: that is, listening out for the sounds within words. Rhymes, rhyming stories and alliteration are excellent ways of encouraging phonemic awareness.

In this story, your child will soon identify the *e* sound, as in **Ted** and **shed**. Look out, too, for rhymes such as **see** – **tree** and **nails** – **tails**.

Hearing your child read

If your child is reading a story to you, don't rush to correct mistakes, but be ready to prompt or guide if he or she is struggling. Above all, give plenty of praise and encouragement.